Parents and Caregivers,

Here are a few ways to support your beginning reader:

- Talk with your child about the ideas addressed in the story.
- Discuss each illustration, mentioning the characters, where they are, and what they are doing.
- Read with expression, pointing to each word.
- Talk about why the character did what he or she did and what your child would do in that situation.
- Help your child connect with characters and events in the story.

Remember, reading with your child should be fun, not forced.

Gail Saunders-Smith, Ph.D

Padres y personas que cuidan niños,

Aquí encontrarán algunas formas de apoyar al lector que recién se inicia:

- Hable con su niño/a sobre las ideas desarrolladas en el cuento.
- Discuta cada ilustración, mencionando los personajes, dónde se encuentran y qué están haciendo.
- Lea con expresión, señalando cada palabra.
- Hable sobre por qué el personaje hizo lo que hizo y qué haría su niño/a en esa situación.
- Ayude al niño/a a conectarse con los personajes y los eventos del cuento.

Recuerde, leer con su hijo/a debe ser algo divertido, no forzado.

Gail Saunders-Smith, Ph.D

BILINGUAL STONE ARCH READERS

are published by Stone Arch Books, a Capstone imprint
17101 Roe Crest Drive, North Mankato, Minnesota 56003.
www.capstonepub.com

Library of Congress Cataloging-in-Publication data is available on the
Library of Congress website.

ISBN: 978-1-4342-3779-8 (hardcover)
ISBN: 978-1-4342-3918-1 (paperback)

Art Director: Bob Lentz
Graphic Designer: Hilary Wacholz
Original Translation: Claudia Heck
Translation Services: Strictly Spanish
Reading Consultants: Gail Saunders-Smith, Ph.D; Melinda Melton Crow, M.Ed;
Laurie K. Holland, Media Specialist

Printed in the United States of America in Stevens Point, Wisconsin.
102011   006404WZS12

LA NOCHE DE TERROR
THE SCARY NIGHT

Un cuento sobre Robot y Rico

A Robot and Rico Story

por/by **Anastasia Suen**
ilustrado por/illustrated by **Mike Laughead**

STONE ARCH BOOKS
a capstone imprint

This is ROBOT. Robot has lots of tools. He uses the tools to help his best friend, Rico.

Este es ROBOT. Robot tiene muchas herramientas. Él usa las herramientas para ayudar a su mejor amigo, Rico.

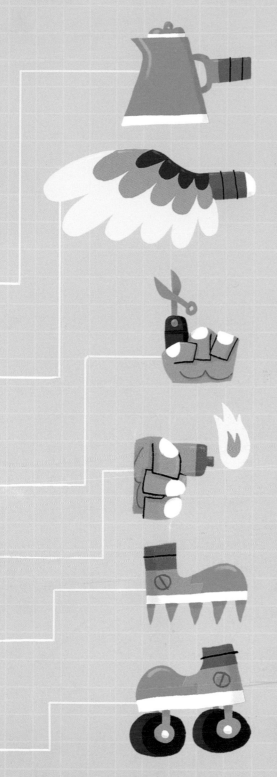

Teapot/
Tetera

Wings/
Alas

Scissors/
Tijeras

Fire Finger/
Dedo de fuego

Special Shoes/
Zapatos especiales

Roller Skates/
Patines con ruedas

"This is a good spot," says Rico.
"I'll put up the tent," says Robot.

"Este es un buen lugar", dice Rico.
"Armaré la carpa", dice Robot.

"I'll find wood," says Rico. "Then we can make a fire."
"And eat," says Robot.

"Buscaré madera", dice Rico.
"Así después podemos hacer
una fogata".
"Y comer", dice Robot.

"This goes here," says Robot.
"And that goes there. Done."

"Esto va aquí", dice Robot.
"Y esto va allá. Listo".

"I have wood for a fire," says Rico.

"Tengo madera para una fogata",
dice Rico.

Robot starts the fire. Robot and Rico cook their hot dogs.

Robot prende la fogata. Robot y Rico cocinan sus hot dogs.

"It's dark in the woods," says Robot.
"I can tell a story," says Rico.

"Está oscuro en el bosque", dice Robot.
"Puedo contarte un cuento",
dice Rico.

"What kind of story?" asks Robot.
"A scary story," says Rico.

"¿Qué tipo de cuento?" pregunta
Robot.
"Un cuento de terror", dice Rico.

"In the deep dark woods," says
Rico, "there is a monster."

"En lo profundo del bosque oscuro",
dice Rico, "vive un monstruo".

peludo

"The monster is big and hairy,"
says Rico.
"Oh, scary," says Robot.

"El monstruo es grande y peludo",
dice Rico.
"Oh, qué miedo", dice Robot.

14

"His name is Big Foot," says Rico. "He has really big feet."

"Su nombre es Pie Grande", dice Rico. "Él tiene pies bien grandes".

"The monster only comes out at night,"
says Rico.
"Why?" asks Robot.

"El monstruo solo sale de noche",
dice Rico.
"¿Por qué?" dice Robot.

"That's when he eats," says Rico.
"What does he eat?" asks Robot.

"Es cuando come", dice Rico.
"¿Qué come?" pregunta Robot.

17

"Everything," says Rico.
"Wow," says Robot.

"De todo", dice Rico.
"Ay", dice Robot.

18

"Big Foot hides in the trees,"
says Rico. "Then he jumps!"

"Pie Grande se esconde en los
árboles", dice Rico. "¡ Y luego
salta!"

"That is a scary story," says Robot.

"Ese sí es un cuento de terror",
dice Robot.

"The fire is out," says Rico.
"We can go to sleep now."

"Se apagó el fuego", dice Rico.
"Podemos dormirnos ahora".

Robot and Rico go into the tent.
They hear a loud noise. Snap!

Robot y Rico entran en la carpa.
Escuchan un ruido fuerte. ¡Snap!

"It's Big Foot!" says Rico.

"¡Es Pie Grande!" dice Rico.

Robot turns on his light.
"It's just a mouse," says Rico.

Robot enciende la luz.
"Es solo un ratón", dice Rico.

Crack!

Robot turns off his light. They hear another loud noise. Crack!
"It's Big Foot!" says Rico.

Robot apaga la luz. Escuchan otro ruido fuerte. ¡Crack!
"¡Es Pie Grande!" dice Rico.

Robot turns on his light.
"It's just a rabbit," says Rico.

Robot enciende la luz.
"Es solo un conejo", dice Rico.

Robot turns off his light. They hear
another loud noise. Whoooo!
"It's Big Foot!" says Rico.

Robot apaga la luz. Escuchan otro
ruido fuerte. ¡Oooo!
"¡Es Pie Grande!" dice Rico.

27

Robot turns on his light.
"It's just an owl," says Rico.

Robot enciende su luz.
"Es solo un búho", dice Rico.

"Robot, can you please leave the
light on?" asks Rico.
"Sure," says Robot.

"Robot, ¿Puedes dejar la luz encendida
por favor?" pregunta Rico.
"Seguro", dice Robot.

"Good night, Rico," says Robot.
"Good night, Robot," says Rico.

"Buenas noches, Rico", dice Robot.
"Buenas noches, Robot", dice Rico.

30

story words

| tent | fire | monster |
| wood | scary | light |

palabras del cuento

| carpa | fogata | monstruo |
| madera | terror | luz |